Death and Deceit

Val Wingrove

Pen Press

First published in Great Britain by Pen Press

All paper used in the printing of this book has been made
from wood grown in managed, sustainable forests.

ISBN13: 978-1-907499-04-3

Printed and bound in the UK
Pen Press is an imprint of Indepenpress Publishing
Limited
25 Eastern Place
Brighton
BN2 1GJ

A catalogue record of this book is available from
the British Library

Cover design by Jacqueline Abromeit

To my family

For Judy

Love

Val x

In secret we meet
In silence I grieve
That thy heart could forget
Thy spirit deceive
If I should meet thee
After long years
How should I greet thee?
With silence and tears!

Lord Byron (1788 – 1824)

Foreword

Thousands of people each day put themselves into a situation that decides their fate. In doing so, they don't use logic or intelligence, what they use are their emotions.

What their heart is telling them.

It's called human nature.

By putting your fate in someone else's hands, you are giving over to them all of your trust.

More often than not it leads to pain and disaster.

Each person's destiny lies in their own hands, the discovery is that, instead of blaming someone else for what happens, you take responsibility for your own decisions.

Preface

Anna had always been aware of how the sky, sea and fire seemed to bond together, how they mesmerised.

It must have something to do with their dangerous elements but there is also a deeply soothing quality when watching all three. The feeling of peace one has when sitting on the sand, listening and watching the lapping of the waves.

To be sat by a blazing fire looking into the flames creating pictures. Anna truly believed there was nothing so beautiful, and uplifting, as a golden sunset; to see the pink, purple and gold blend together, just before the blackness falls, was a feeling of pure joy.

Sitting on her terrace, listening to the lapping waves and watching the sun slowly descend behind the mountains, a glow like fire rising up into the Mediterranean sky, Anna was feeling all of these moods but soon it would be over, nothing lasts.

Maro

It was March and there was still a chill in the evening air as Anna knew there would be; she had left a London bathed in winter sunshine, giving the city an almost clean appearance, but she was pleased to leave. Anna knew that it was time, David, a long time friend and artist had agreed to look after the gallery for six months, she knew that it would be longer but had neglected to tell him as much.

For the past year Anna had been putting her affairs in order. Her finances were such that she really didn't need to work at all, she was fortunate; or unfortunate as the case may be.

Her caretaker Vincente and his wife Mia had, as usual on her instructions, cleaned and stocked the villa. Standing on the terrace with a chilled glass of Navara wine in her hand, Anna looked across to her right, and could see the twinkling lights of Nerja, and thought that in a few days she would venture into town, but for the moment she was content to enjoy the peace and solitude of her beautiful home.

The villa was set on a precipice overhanging Maro beach and to Anna's eyes had the most spectacular scenery in Southern Spain, with undisturbed views of the Sierra Tejada mountains, and a never-ending vista of the sea. When she had bought the property 10 years previously it had seemed an extortionate amount for the villa, but in her opinion the pleasure she had received since had more than paid for it.

The house was so luxurious, with the eye of an artist Anna had made it so, she had created her masterpiece.

Entering through the black iron gates, the double doors of the villa are a short drive away.

Through these, you are met by the cool entrance of the marbled atrium, with two floors of rooms all interconnecting. The ground floor bedrooms all with the same white highly polished marble, and the rooms above, a peach glow; a feeling of space and comfort blending each room with the next. The walls are pure white so as not to detract from the magnificent paintings Anna had collected over the years.

In the living area overlooking the terrace and sea, the furnishings are in natural shades of cream and beige, with a huge fire at one end of the room, and two large comfortable chairs facing each other in front of it.

Three cream settees with a 5ft coffee table at the other end finished the room. Anna came in from the terrace and placed the still chilled bottle of wine on the small table beside one of the fireside chairs, settling, she allowed the warmth of the flames wash over her, and a smile slowly rises from her lips and reaches her eyes. Suddenly, laughter bubbled up from deep inside her and, for a full 30 seconds real joyful laughter filled the villa. Mia from the kitchen stopped preparing dinner and listened, thinking it was good to hear Anna laugh. But if she had seen Anna at that moment, she would have seen the laughter turn to tears, tears that for a time she thought would never end, tears that had been a long time coming, now were here, the heart breaking sobs that seemed as though they would never stop.

The thought that hammered in her brain as she tried desperately to control herself, was that she would have to write it down; tell Belle what had happened. It was impossible to hold it in and Belle would know what to do in the end. Belle would have to inherit the bad with the good; whatever she wished to do with the knowledge was her decision, *at least I will have purged myself*, Anna thought. Having decided this Anna felt a sudden calm, a shudder came from her whole body. Relieved from the tension, she looked around her as though for the first time since arriving and said, "I'm home, home to die." As she watched the flames, her thoughts returned to her childhood.

Anna Draycott's early life had been ideal; her parents only child, she was cherished and loved, but from the time she could talk, her father had taken it upon himself to introduce her to his private passion, 'The Arts'. To his delight she soaked up everything and it was a joy when they visited The National Gallery or the Tate to try and answer her many questions.

When Anna was a teenager, she would accompany Oliver and Joan, her parents, to gallery openings and she became quite conversant in all aspects of art. Those who knew the family just took her intelligence as the norm and would speak to her as an equal.

When Anna started art college she thought all of her dreams had come true, but soon was to realise that although technically very good, her paintings would only ever be described as proficient. Belle her best friend, said she was mad to leave the course, but Anna decided not to waste any more of her parents' money, and with the connections she had made in the art world, found a position at a gallery just off Bond Street.

Learning everything that was needed to run a successful business did not always come easily, but the enthusiasm she demonstrated won over all who met her.

"*Señorita* Anna!" She heard the call from Mia, dinner was ready; tomorrow she would tell them what was going on and hoped they would understand! Drying her eyes and lifting the bottle of wine she walked toward the kitchen and Mia's delicious meal, knowing full well she would be unable to do the food justice.

Earlier that day after Vincente had left for the airport. Mia had sat preparing the vegetables for the evening meal in the sunshine by the kitchen door, musing to herself about how lucky they had been.

It was 10 years since Anna had bought the villa, and had saved their home.

Vincente and Mia worked for the previous owner for almost 20 years; they had lived in their small *finca* within the grounds of the property since the day they had married. Both worked hard; Vincente on the land and Mia caring for the family, preparing meals and cleaning, she was always on hand when needed. When the old landlord died, his children decided to sell everything and their mother went to live with the eldest in Madrid. It was a great blow to Mia who had become more of a companion to the *Señora* after the death of her husband.

When the viewings started, Mia would make sure everything in the villa was sparkling, but for some it was not enough. Listening to the comments as the visitors walked through the building she would sometimes have to bite her tongue, "Oh; I think we would have to knock it down..."

"We would definitely have to remove most of the trees..."

"I suppose we could turn that funny little house into games room..." were just a few of the things she overheard. It was very frightening, so Mia and Vincente decided that when the time finally came they would move to an apartment in the village; then one cold day in January, Anna arrived.

There had been so many false starts and Mia was, after six months of cleaning the soulless villa, despairing of the family ever finding a buyer, so when Anna walked through the gate, Mia eyed her with a look of boredom, *another timewaster, far to young to be able to afford this*; but the tall, pale, auburn-haired English woman was to surprise her.

The news came about a week after Anna's visit that an offer had been made on the property, a shocked Vincent and Mia now realised they were virtually homeless, it was difficult for them to comprehend.

When Anna returned for a second and more in-depth look around, Mia was introduced to her. Neither could speak the others language and they had to resort to the agent for interpretation. Anna asked all sorts of questions about their life and seemed genuinely interested in her replies.

That evening, when Vincente returned from the fields expecting to find a morbid and morose Mia there was a surprise awaiting him, his wife turned from her preparation of the evening meal as he entered the *finca* and smiled. Listening to Mia's renewed views of the lady who was going live in the Villa, he wondered why she was so cheerful; after all, what had changed? Nothing; surely they would still have to leave, but no; Mia wanted him to listen; the English lady wished for them to stay! Ten years had passed and now Anna had told them; I'm coming home for good! *This is a happy day*, Mia thought, as she walked over to the herb garden and picked the basil for tonight's meal.

London

Looking at the crushed skull of the man lying on the stainless steel trolley in the morgue, Tim Walters could only think, *what a waste; someone with so much and who should have had at least another 50 years ahead of him, what a waste!*

This was going to be a real pig of an investigation; Inspector Walters could feel it in the pit of his stomach as soon as he had received the call that a body had been discovered at the Tower Hotel and it was definitely no accident. Of course the hotel wanted to keep everything extremely quiet; nothing like this had ever happened before, but unfortunately for them it was not to be. The police weren't too pleased either, where the hell to start, with hundreds of people floating in and out of the place?

It was imperative they identify the victim. He had signed into the hotel as J Baird, but the driver's licence said Michael G Foley, the address the prestigious Chelsea Harbour.

On booking the double room for two nights he had asked not to be disturbed.

The clerk on duty that afternoon remembered looking up and thinking Mr Baird looked tired but really he had not taken too much notice. Yes, Mr Baird had been unaccompanied and no one had requested his room number.

Walters still thought he must have been meeting someone probably a woman; why else book a hotel room a couple of miles from where you lived? Why not meet at your home? All of these details needed to be sorted out, his minions could do the leg work, and it should only take a matter of hours to get a full history on Michael G Foley; at least in theory that's how it should work.

The room which was 12ft square with en suite bathroom, dressing table and a long stool on which sat his overnight bag. Foley had been found by the chambermaid, lying at the foot of the bed. Nothing seemed to have been disturbed and his overnight bag was still unpacked. The police pathologist estimated at the scene that his life had been extinguished around 16 hours previously. Once forensics had taken photographs of the scene and completely dusted everything, the body was removed and the room was then sealed.

Walters hated having to go to the mortuary, he could never come to terms with seeing human life laid bare, but for all that, he stood and watched as the pathologist described how Foley died.

It had been one massive blow to the head; someone with great strength and anger. The murder weapon had not been found at the scene.

More would be learned later about the angle and height, which would help in identifying how tall the murderer was but for now it seemed to look like a random killing.

On his way back to the office the inspector wondered if Nobby Clarke, his sergeant, had managed to find anything out about the man's background, what was so bloody annoying was that whoever was responsible had 16 hours to cover their tracks.

*

David Jacks entered the gallery at 10am, it was still very cold but April would soon be here and with it the first signs of spring. He was in a buoyant mood, still on a high and he had Anna to thank.

It had been a pleasant surprise when three weeks previously she had telephoned and invited him for dinner at her apartment above the gallery. He had been extremely busy in the last three months tying to complete a series of nudes in aquarelle for an exhibition at the Eton gallery he was affiliated to and his friend Mark had taken the last painting to be framed, so the invitation could not have come at a better time.

He walked down the King's Road with a spring in his step, enjoying the sense of relief that only comes from having completed something for once, on time.

When Anna answered the buzzer at his first ring David pushed the door, making sure it was firmly closed behind him he bounced up the two flights of stairs expecting to see the stunning, statuesque Anna waiting at the top. The door was askew and Anna called out from the kitchen to pour a glass of wine and make him-self comfortable; he was more than pleased to acquiesce. He knew the wine would be Spanish but he didn't mind, they seemed to have adapted to European tastes in the past 10 years, and were a lot more palatable than people realised. Anna had a love of anything Spanish. Although her apartment was sparsely furnished it had been done in the most exquisite taste and it was always a pleasure to slowly walk around the 30ft living dining room and appreciate the artists she had collected, some of whom were still unknown to the majority of the art world, but all with unquestionable talent; Anna definitely had an eye for seeing who had true talent and who might just be a one canvas wonder.

David remembered thinking how slightly envious he had been that none of his own work was displayed, then, he remembered Anna saying the one painting she possessed of his hung above her bed; it being too erotic for the living room. He wondered what the hell was keeping her so long, and although the smells from the kitchen were delicious, it really was *Anna* he had come to see. Suddenly she was standing before him; she had caught him off guard, looking at the expression on his face it was as though she could read his mind.

"No need to say it! I know what I look like! I haven't been too well lately and I'm feeling a bit run down," but David stood completely still in shock, until he realised how rude his staring was. Anna was laughing at his expression and he immediately went to her and gave her a huge hug, feeling a shadow of her former self in his arms. It didn't seem possible for someone to change so much in such a short time.

David suddenly became really worried, he asked Anna to tell him what was wrong; but she was dismissive, only saying that she had had a few woman's problems, knowing it would shut him up at once. She said she was recovering but needed to ask him a favour.

Over a sumptuous dinner, which Anna barely touched, she had told him her doctor had advised complete rest for at least six months. She knew he had just completed his latest series and she wondered if he would think it too much of an imposition for him to look after the gallery. Now it was his turn to laugh. The look in her eyes told him she was serious, he said yes without thinking but knew that at that moment, anything she asked of him, the reply would have been *yes*. That had been three weeks ago, and he had been looking after the gallery one week, everything was going like clockwork. There was an exhibition to prepare in a month's time, but Anna's staff of two, Trish and Pat, had assured him it was all in hand and he was really enjoying chatting to the passing trade and buyers who came to browse.

When Belle returned from a buying trip to the States and read Anna's letter, she was more surprised than shocked, she knew Anna had been going through a bad time physically and had become very run down, but Belle thought it would only be a matter of weeks before her friend was back to her normal exuberant self.

For Anna to take a full six months away from the gallery was unheard of, she had left instructions with Belle to contact David on her return, he would be staying in the apartment and looking after the gallery full-time, Belle phoned him immediately and arranged to see him the following day, then, still a bit jet lagged, she fell into bed and was almost asleep before her head hit the pillow.

*

It was five days since the body had been found. They had discovered that Michael Foley was a bachelor living alone in a two bed, two bathroom apartment at Chelsea Harbour and he worked for an Asset Management company in the city.

Sergeant Nobby Clarke had been given the job of going through the man's personal effects. On entering the apartment, his first reaction had been a low whistle and the thought, *so this is how the other half live*; the cool black and white tiles led from the vestibule into a living area that must have been 20ft plus, with large windows looking down onto a courtyard, the furniture was huge and comfortable. Away from the main seating area, under a beautiful Paul Kenny landscape was a large bureau. Sergeant Clarke decided to start with that, perhaps Foley was as neat with his personal effects as with his apartment.

The bureau was locked, searching through the keys in his possession Sergeant Clarke hoped he wouldn't have to break into the lovely piece of furniture. He found the small brass key and inserted it into the lock. Papers were laid in neat bundles on the writing surface and each drawer seemed to be overflowing with correspondence; he had a feeling it was going to be a long job. Taking everything from the bureau he settled on one of the leather settees and prepared himself for a long afternoon.

Michael G Foley looked from outer appearances to be the man who had everything. His work colleagues were slightly envious, how did Mike do it? Thirty five years old, and still single, why had some clever young girl not snapped him up? He was

5ft 11 inches tall, dark hair, blue eyes that seemed to have a cheeky twinkle in them when chatting to all the young secretaries, he wore a permanent tan throughout the year, he was always pleasant and good natured, the men at the office thought he had it made, the women would drool and wonder who the lucky girl was. What was unusual was that no one at his work knew anything about his personal life.

Maro

The white bodies lay on the dark volcanic sand in the daily ritual of offering themselves to the sun god, their brain-dead owners giving themselves over to yet another day of exhausting, thirst inducing sunbathing.

It was the first day of April and Anna was sitting in the shade of Marino's Bar sipping a tinto verana. Temperatures had reached an all time high for that time of year and the beach bars were extremely busy.

Driving back from Velez-Malaga after her appointment with the specialist, Anna had decided to detour down to Burriana Beach, she enjoyed the anonymity of the large beach, being alone yet surrounded by the low hum of voices, snippets of conversation reaching the ears, guttural Germans, shouting Italians, arrogant French, dull English; she wondered not for the first time how all of these nationalities had managed to discover this gem of Spain, couldn't blame all of it on Judith Chalmers' travel show.

The doctor had been very courteous and gentle with her, reading through her medical history he had assured her of his total discretion and said he was at her disposal day or night. When asked if she would like a live in nurse; Anna had declined; perhaps later, nearer the time.

Anna's weight had dropped from her usual 9½ stone to 8 stone, she knew her appearance was verging on anorexic but until she could no longer fend for herself, she wished to lead as normal a life as possible. A peace had settled on her after that first night. She no longer thought of the weeks preceding her arrival; anger, fear, abolished from her mind, the only thought she had at that moment was, *why is that hugely obese woman parading around with only bikini bottoms on, and would they ever employ beach police to tell people with really sagging boobs and ugly fat stomachs to cover up or leave, as police in the South of France apparently do?*

Anna decided to stay a little longer and indulge in her favourite pastime. People-watching, somehow it was easier here in Spain, everyone seemed to stare without embarrassment at everyone else, it helped wearing dark glasses. A young couple deep in conversation; were passing the bar, on the man's back was something that resembled a rucksack and sitting neatly into it was a child of about 18 months, and tightly held in it's tiny hand, a large runny ice cream, Anna could tell what was going to happen before it did, as the mother continued talking and walking, the father stood stock still, the delicious cold ice running down the back of his neck, it was only a matter of seconds before the woman realised what had happened but by then everyone in the bar was laughing, including Anna.

London

When Belle lunched with David the day following her return from the States, they discussed Anna's appearance. Although Belle had not seen her for six weeks, she had assumed her friend's health would have improved. David told her Anna looked like a bag of bones and on that one invitation to dinner had barely touched her food.

Belle knew better than to get in contact with Anna, they had been best friends since school and although totally different personalities; were closer than sisters. So when she said she was having a complete break then that was exactly what she meant. Belle told David if he needed anything at all to give her a call, perhaps they could have dinner the following week when she wasn't so busy.

When Sir Geoffrey Tyne was told, all he could do was shake his head. But it's impossible, "Why? How?", Inspector Walters had to take him through it yet another time, Mr Foley had been found murdered at the Tower Hotel, they had been unable to trace any relatives; and did Sir Geoffrey or any of his staff know of anyone who was close to the deceased man?

This so-called intelligent man was stretching Walters' patience to the limit, how many more times did he need to be told that Foley had passed on, become extinct; was no more; this interview was in serious danger of reverting to a Monty Python sketch! Finally, Sir Geoffrey buzzed for his secretary and asked her to call into his office, those who had worked closest to Mike; *about time*, Walters was thinking, *at last a bit of action*, but he was to be disappointed. Although Foley had worked at the brokerage firm for five years, no one had become close to him outside the office, it wasn't for the want of trying, but he would always decline politely when invited to the wine bar for a drink, so in the end they just gave up asking him.

Walters thanked the staff and Sir Geoffrey dismissed them. The police had been unable to find any personal letters in Foley's apartment and the body had as yet to be formally identified, so Inspector Walters suggested to Sir Geoffrey if he could possibly spare an hour at the end of his working day, it would be very much appreciated by the police if he would identify the body, Sir Geoffrey went puce in colour. "Is it absolutely necessary?"

"I'm afraid so since, no relatives have been traced also there seem to have been a lot of documents pertaining to his work which you might want to collect from the station." At the mention of these, Sir Geoffrey stiffened and his stare became sharp; Sir Geoffrey Tyne had a terrible premonition that today was the start of a very sticky patch for the brokerage firm of Tyne Weller and Munch.

There must have been over a hundred phone numbers in Michael Foley's book. Sergeant Clark had the job of deciphering the personal numbers from the business numbers. Taken that most had been entered by their initials it was proving an extremely long and boring venture. Anna's entry in Michael's phone book was listed as A. D Galleries, so was promptly put in the business file to be dealt with at a later date.

"Take it from me, this bloke is going to turn out to be a weirdo, no family, and from what we have gathered so far, no one who wants to claim him as a friend." Inspector Walters was speaking to his Sergeant, "and I'm not sure we should have allowed Sir Geoffrey to take those papers; did you see the expression on his face when he was looking through them? If anything, it was whiter than when he saw Foley lying on the slab."

Foley was turning into an enigma for Walters. They had discovered he had been born just outside Liverpool, his parents died when he was 16 years old and he had moved in with his mother's aunt. It seemed they were not a family who had found the elixir of life, Foley had just finished at an obscure university when his aunt died and he moved down to London, seemingly having no trouble getting a job in one of the major brokerage houses. He had been poached by Sir Geoffrey's firm five years previously and that was as far as they got. Walters believed no man lived for work alone and Foley had created enough emotion in at least one person, he was dead after all, Sergeant Clarke was voicing out loud his thoughts on Foley's apartment about how well he had lived.

"He has some really nice pictures on the walls sir." Inspector Walters suddenly had an idea, taking his coat from the rack he told Clark to bring the car around, they were going to have another look at Michael Foley's apartment, again, this case was getting under his skin and he wanted it cleared up before his holiday in May; his wife had told him she wouldn't cancel anymore holidays because of the pressure of his job; and if need be, she would go alone. Not that he thought she would, but he didn't want to take any chances.

On looking through the papers at the police station, Sir Geoffrey's fears had been confirmed; he had tried to keep his persona calm in front of the two officers but could feel the sick stirrings and shaking start as he signed the release form. He went straight back to his office, it was eight in the evening, phoning his two partners, he told them both to get there immediately. The shit was really going to hit the fan; unless they could come up with some sort of plan.

Maro

Anna's days had taken on a gentle routine. Leaving home at 10 in the morning, she drove into Nerja, parking at the top of the town; she would meander down Calle Pintada, taking her time, looking at the bright array of goods in the shop windows.

All roads lead to Rome, so the saying goes. In Nerja, all roads lead to the Balcon de Europe, Anna's ritual would take her to the end of the Balcon where she would stand for a few moments enjoying the calm, peaceful scene at this still early hour.

Having finished her promenade, she would then walk to the Plaza Cabana Hotel, situated just behind the 16th century El Salvador church, there she would order a *café con leche* and watch the town slowly come to life. Feeling a part of the new day yet separated from the lives of these people, most would pass and give her a quick nod and a smile, knowing her face but not knowing from where. Occasionally

Anna caught a glimpse of headlines from English newspapers but she would quickly turn away, allowing nothing to disturb her feeling of inner peace.

Looking at her life as a whole, would she have led a less selfish existence if by a twist of fate her parents had not died in that car crash? There was no point in 'what ifs'. She had loved both her parents very deeply and they had given her a wonderful childhood. When they died just before her 23rd birthday, part of her also died. With the money left to her from her father. Anna joined forces with Charles Boyd. Charles had been a friend of the family and when she suggested to him that she would like to invest in his gallery and perhaps go around the country scouting for new artists, he was delighted. It would take a load off his shoulders and give Anna some purpose. Anna had been like a breath of fresh air to the gallery, full of energy and ideas, and the once staid business started to come to life with her help.

Making her way back home, Anna remembered Mia and Vincente's reaction when she told them her situation. Mia had immediately broken down into tears, whilst Vincente, reaching for her hand and kissing it, said they would both be there for her to do anything she needed. She had been grateful beyond belief, not thinking until that moment how she would have missed these two dear friends. At five she awakened from her siesta and sipped the tea Mia had laid out for her on the bedside table, the birds outside were the only sound she heard, she could visualise them flitting back and forth to the church roof, feeding their young nesting in the terracotta tiles.

Tonight she would take her dear friends to the Detunda restaurant, just a small thank you for their understanding and support.

Vincente could always make her laugh with his farmyard humour and although Mia would tut she would end up giggling throughout the meal.

London

On their way to Foley's place, Sergeant Clarke mentioned to his boss the fact that he, Clarke had photocopied every piece of paper taken from Foley's apartment. Inspector Walters gave him an appreciative glance. "So we can have a closer look at the documents Sir Geoffrey seemed so frightened about; good."

Entering the apartment, the officers looked at each other in surprise, they could hear in a distant room the sound of someone humming and the post had been placed neatly on the vestibule table, quietly they made their way to where the sound was coming from.

The cleaning woman looked up and let our a soft yelp, the Inspector held up his hand and announced that they were the police, the woman told them in no uncertain terms that they had frightened the life out of her; finally, when she had calmed down, they ascertained that she was employed by a cleaning company to clean apartments in the block once a month on a rota basis.

There were 10 cleaners in all and this had been her second visit in this particular apartment in the past 12 months, and she was quick to point out that it was a hell of a lot cleaner than some she had to clean.

They asked her if she had ever seen the owner or met anyone when she cleaned it the last time, but her reply was no. *Another dead end* Walters was thinking. Glancing around the bedroom, his attention was drawn to the painting above the bed, it depicted a naked man, a horse and a dog, painted in deep blues and mauves, there was something very erotic about it and he found himself slightly disturbed the longer he stared. He didn't know it, but the painting was a very fine example of Lin Jammet's work, Anna had been hoping the artist would one day exhibit at her gallery but his affiliation with others had unfortunately made it a far-off project.

With the cleaning woman gone, Walters had moved into the living room, he felt more comfortable here, the bedroom had an oppressive air about it, but this room with its large leather sofas and solid wood furniture was more to his taste.

He was sure, looking at the paintings which bedecked the three walls, there was yet another side to Foley not that he had managed to discover much. On an impulse he told Clarke to remove the paintings from the walls and turn them around, Sergeant Clarke looked askance but did what he was told. Looking at the back of each in turn, Inspector Walters nodded and wrote notes in his book. He wrote for quite a long time taking care to put the details down correctly, there were three Paul Kenny, two Solani, one Kingsley, one Roman Francis and two McDonald all acquired from the same gallery, going back to the bedroom, he looked at the back of the Lin Jammit, took down the details and replaced it.

Just before leaving the apartment, Sergeant Clarke looked at the post, and he left everything except the phone bill. He hoped to correlate the numbers with those in Foley's book and see who he had spoken to on the days preceding his death.

The offices of Tyne, Weller and Munch were a hive of activity; Tony Bolt had been asked by his boss Peter Day to collect from the computer every transaction Mike Foley had completed in his five years at the firm, it was proving to be a major task and he had to ask for two people to help him.

Sir Geoffrey Tyne was having palpitations during his meeting with the partners; a few harsh criticisms had come his way. It did not feel good to be on the receiving end of their wrath, he had been told bluntly the ball was in his court and he had better sort out the mess or certain heads would roll.

He knew of course that if rumours of insider trading were to leak, it would immediately be assumed he had a hand in it.

Before leaving his home for the Tyne office, Martin Weller, one of the partners, entered an upstairs room at his home and removed every item of evidence that might prove he had had any personal knowledge of Michael Foley. Munch, the third partner of the firm, had retired 12 years previously. His mantel had been assumed by Sir Brian Dunne, he could not understand Tyne's panic; surely his death was no concern of theirs? Of course he knew Foley had been a high flyer with the firm and that he had set up the Hedge fund department but if he chose to get himself killed in some hotel room, what could they do about it?

After listening to Sir Geoffrey's account of what had occurred earlier, Martin Weller's mind was racing, he was the type of person who always thought the best line of defence was attack. He knew a few of the names in the document Geoffrey had shown them, he also knew he would have to warn them that they were about to be exposed.

Outwardly calm, he asked Sir Geoffrey what he intended to do about the situation. Once he saw him start to bluster he knew he had the upper hand. Sir Geoffrey had expected both partners to give him some support in this, but Weller informed him Foley had been his man, *he* was the one who had poached him, he declined to mention it was at his instigation, Weller couldn't wait to get out of the office, he needed to make those calls. The police would obviously be delving deep into Foley's past and he was praying nothing would point to him or the others. They needed to be prepared to get their stories straight.

Inspector Walters was grateful Clarke had copied the documents, but he really couldn't make head or tail of them, he needed someone who knew about the financial market to look them over. He decided to show them to a friend of his in the fraud squad; it wouldn't hurt to know what they were about. At that moment if Sir Geoffrey had known what was going through the policeman's mind, his heart might have given out.

One of the numbers listed on the telephone bill from Foley's apartment matched that for A. D. Gallery; fortunately most of the calls made were the same numbers on different days, Sergeant Clarke cross-filed these against those on his list, two numbers kept repeating, M.W and A. D. Gallery.

He made a note to interview both within the next day or two.

Things were getting a bit hectic around the gallery, David hadn't quite realised how much work was involved in putting on an exhibition, Trish had sent out all the invitations a month ago, but the artist, a rather laid-back Scot had yet to deliver his final four paintings. David knew that at least one of them was in the catalogue, frustrated, he was thinking, why couldn't the artist organise himself better? Then he pulled himself up short, he could remember sending gallery owners into fits of frenzy by not delivering until the very morning of the show.

Belle had promised to attend and help out if need be; she had told him not to worry,

Anna had always said it was just like giving a cocktail party, just make sure the drink flows and you have a few nibbles to pass around. She had another piece of advice and that was to make sure he didn't give 'the Scot' too much to drink, keep him moving around the room talking to people, it seemed when he had a few he tended to fall over, Belle had seen it happen. David was frightened Anna would have no credibility left by the time she came home.

Entering the shop the two officers were faced with a scene from a farce, the man up the ladder was precariously hanging onto a large painting, the expression on his face was verging between tears and fear, he was screaming to someone called Pat to hold the stepladder, declaring he had a fear of heights and he should have got that bloody Scot to hang his own paintings. It was the morning of the exhibition and the artist had strolled into the gallery at 9am, left his four paintings and strolled out again with an aside that he would be back at 5 o'clock. David caught sight of the two men who had just entered, he was just about to say the gallery was closed until the afternoon, when his hand slipped and the painting slew to one side, he let out a sharp cry. The smaller of the two men was beside him and before he had time to realise what was happening the painting was being held up waiting to be secured.

Having eventually managed to hang the offending article, David descended from the ladder, small beads of sweat had formed on his forehead, he thanked Sergeant Clarke for his help; the sergeant in turn introduced himself and the inspector.

Describing the scene later to Belle, David tried to recollect everything the police officers had said.

"Apparently, a chap called Michael Foley has been found murdered and they were talking to everyone who had contact with him; he had about 9 or 10 paintings bought from here and they wanted to know if I knew Mr Foley well."

Belle asked him what he had told the police and he said nothing because it wasn't until after they had left that he realised who Michael Foley was and he had told them that the owner of the gallery was abroad for six months recuperating from an illness. Belle felt a sense of relief, relief that Anna was not here to learn of his death, the man had caused her friend too much pain already.

She could recall his face as plainly as though it were yesterday they had just met;

he had pleasant features and an open smile, a smile that had belied the bastard behind it. Each time she thought of Michael Foley which fortunately these days was rare, a cold rage would sweep over her on her friends behalf. Over four years had passed since Anna had become besotted with Foley; they had been together a long six months. Once he had entrapped her with his easy manner, he then proceeded to degrade and destroy her confidence, if it had not been for the fact that Anna had strong-minded friends who kept telling her she was being used as well as abused, and consequently her own personality was changing. Belle was sure her friend would have had a complete mental breakdown. In the end Anna found the courage to break all contact with Foley, she went to her beloved Spain for a month and returned a much stronger person, although Belle suspected she had never fully recovered from the experience.

Belle said to David "If the police should return, say you know nothing," which in truth he didn't, at that moment the first patrons were arriving and David was thinking *where the hell is 'the Scot'?* thoughts of the police and Foley banished from his mind.

*

It was only a month until his supposed holiday and Inspector Walters was beginning to panic. He had gotten nowhere with his investigation and couldn't see any clear leads falling into his lap in the very near future. Sitting in The Old Crown waiting for the arrival of Sammy, his mate from the fraud squad, he was wondering if he should tell the wife to cancel, and book something later in the year. Shaking his head he thought his life would not be worth living if he did.

Sammy entered the pub and giving him a wave, went straight to the bar. He ordered two pints of bitter and brought them to where Walters was sitting by the window. After greeting each other, Sammy came out with his bombshell.

"Well Tim, you've got yourself a nice can of worms haven't you?" Walters looked at him in what could only be described as despair, *what now?* This holiday was looking more and more like a distant dream.

The documents set out in detail the names of people who had received information from an insider trading net going back almost five years they also detailed how much each person had paid for the information.

"All in all," said Sammy, "a nice little case for the fraud team." Walters wanted to know if the Fraud Squad would be taking over the investigation, but Sammy said no; they would have to work hand in hand but should anything or anyone be found that directly connects with Foley, they would do everything to assist Walters. Foley's name had not appeared anywhere in the documents, but the fact that they had been found in his apartment pointed to two probabilities. Firstly that, he had discovered the fraud and was killed to keep him quiet, or, he was part and parcel of the whole set up. Walters was only too pleased to allow Sammy to find out for him. The inspector would have liked to be with Sammy and his men when they entered the offices of Tyne Weller and Munch, he wondered if Sir Geoffrey Tyne was up to his pompous neck in this business, it would be interesting to find out. Sergeant Clarke would go round and collect all the senior partners' alibis for the time when Foley was murdered. It would give him some pleasure to send his minion to interview these men, and he started to feel happier until he thought of his wife.

Maro

Everything had been going really well; the doctor had told Anna her condition was quite stable for the moment and although they both knew it would only last only a short time; she was feeling very optimistic.

Mia had packed her a picnic basket to take to the beach, it was amazing how one small piece of good news had lifted her spirits and allowed her to see things in a different light. Anna thought she must have been going around in a daze for the last five weeks, because suddenly she was able to appreciate the feeling of wellbeing and wonder in this most beautiful, vibrant country.

Parking outside Merino's she looked up at the azure sky. Lowering her eyes, the white villas seemed to glisten under their terracotta roofs; it seemed incongruous that they were able to build at such an obscure angle on the ochre cliff. Picking up her basket, towel and bag, she made her way over the soft volcanic sand; calling the beach boy over, she selected a sun bed close to the back of the shaded area. Keeping the head of the bed under the straw umbrella, Anna settled herself back and contemplated her surroundings. The sea, looking at the waves coming in from the Med, the white foam dancing onto the beach like a million crabs fleeing the waves for fear of being drowned. There were mainly couples and groups of older people sunning themselves at this early hour and everything was calm and quiet, reaching into her bag she removed her book, it was a Boyd novel she had always meant to read, she only hoped she wouldn't laugh too loudly, looking around she thought *what more could anyone want*.

Anna awoke thinking, *My God, What?* The sound assailing her ears was like a banshee, the family had ensconced themselves directly behind her and the mother was screaming at the child to sod off and leave her alone when she was trying to have a *siesta*, the father-who looked like a lump of blubber was lying in a drunken slumber. Anna couldn't believe her eyes or ears, if the woman acted like this in public, what must she be like at home? The child, who looked about 7 years old, was standing just out of smacking distance looking totally miserable as the tirade kept going on and on, and other bathers were beginning to look.

Anna was wondering if she should leave as a natural pacifist it was always easier for her to retreat from unsightly situations, but something came over her. She thought, *I'll be dammed if I'm going to allow this woman to make everyone else feel uncomfortable*. Slowly rising from her bed, she walked over to the fishwife; standing directly in front of the woman and completely blocking out her sun she waited for the mouth to clamp shut, which happened almost immediately.

Bending down, Anna said in her calmest voice, "If you don't keep your mouth shut and stop the foul language, it will be my pleasure to have you removed from this beach." The woman started to protest but Anna stopped her by raising a hand and saying. "It would be no trouble at all for the bed owners to call the local police," turning her back Anna went over to her own bed and with a smile to a few other bathers, settled back to her book. Not a sound was heard from behind her, she couldn't believe what she had just done; a few people were looking at her, their eyes saying *if we could applaud you, we would*. After a late lunch of chicken in a garlic and cucumber sauce and a sweet potato salad she went up to the beach bar for a drink. Manolo, the owner, greeted her with a handshake and kisses on both cheeks. She had known his family since her first year at Maro, had watched his children grow from plump contented babies to cheeky toddlers, to well mannered young children.

The previous year he and his wife had invited her to the communion of his daughter which was a great honour; although she couldn't believe the amount of money they had spent on what should primarily have been a quiet religious ceremony. The dress had been specially made, and any royal bride would have been delighted by the design.

There were at least 100 guests at the party afterwards, the tables groaning under the weight of food, a four-tier cake taking central position at the top table and the children who had been invited with their parents all left with small gifts. Anna had been delighted to share in this very Spanish occasion but had been taken aback by the extravagance of it all.

Chatting with Manolo, she could suddenly see that he was making a special point of speaking to her, the bar was extremely busy yet he was taking time out to sit with her, then she realised what she must look like to him, Anna had been feeling so well lately and with her weight loss slowing down she was so used to what she looked at in the mirror each morning now, that, other people's reactions still surprised her. Manolo told her she needed feeding up; she was getting too skinny, what had happened to Mia's cooking he wanted to know? Leaving the bar with a sudden depression shrouding her thoughts, she decided to go home. A chill had enveloped Anna through the day's growing heat.

London

Telling the names that the game was up, Weller also told them that on no account, was he to be mentioned when speaking to the police. Their best form of defence was to lay everything at Michael Foley's door, what could possibly be wrong in taking advice from someone of his experience? And they were so grateful of course, that it was only natural to give him a gift. Weller knew it was a flimsy line of defence, but he had to make sure none of these men said anything that would incriminate him, he knew he was not mentioned in the documents but if even one man said it was he, Weller, who had introduced Foley to them, the police would be on him like a tonne of bricks.

Sir Geoffrey Tyne seated behind the large teak desk had made his decision. Picking up the telephone, he asked his secretary to get inspector Walters on the phone. When the call came through he asked the inspector if he could come by his office as soon as possible, that done, he sat back with relief. When Walters entered the Tyne offices, he had thought he would find a very worried man, but kept his surprise to himself as Sir Geoffrey came from behind his desk and shook him amicably by the hand saying it was most kind of him to come so promptly. After they were seated and the girl had brought in coffee, Sir Geoffrey told Walters that having read through the documents found at Mike Foley's apartment he had to tell the inspector of his fears of a serious fraud against his firm; they had looked at all Foley's dealings for the past four and half years and there were a lot of discrepancies; it had taken a good three weeks to sort out the mess.

Sir Geoffrey wished to put matters into the hands of the police and give them as much help as he could, there was no way that Tyne could have known the fraud squad were already involved, so Walters thanked Sir Geoffrey and asked if it would be possible to use the phone, might as well get Sammy over there as soon as possible, since they were being invited to investigate the firm by Tyne himself. Sir Geoffrey's partners had put the ball in his court and he had promptly booted it out, after all what had happened was none of his making, why cover it up? Let the police do his job for him, they would soon find out who had been behind Foley and then he, Sir Geoffrey Tyne would go in for the kill.

Belle had no time to worry about Anna's absence, she had been busy at work for the past three months, now that things had calmed down she was feeling guilty, perhaps her friend wouldn't have gone rushing off to Spain if she had been on hand to offer some comfort and support. Anna didn't have a phone at her villa and had always refused to have one installed, she had said it would only disturb the peace and quiet she sought to find when she was there, so Belle decided to write her a long, chatty letter. It wasn't until halfway through it she decided to insert in an offhand way the fact of Michael Foley's death although she found it difficult to be offhand about him even on paper. Trying to keep her tone light, she told Anna of the evening of 'The Scot's' exhibition, and how David had spent an hilarious four hours trying to steer him away from the drinks table; the artist couldn't understand why each time he was just about to pick up a glass, David would suddenly grab hold of his arm and haul him off to speak to yet another client, by the end of the night David was almost in a state of collapse from trying to keep the unsuspecting Scot sober and had needed a stiff drink himself. The blessed relief for him was that the exhibition was completely sold out and it wasn't until the following day he had been able to look at the artists work and really appreciate 'The Scot's' talent. Belle also bemoaned the fact that Anna hadn't once phoned her, and asked her please to keep in touch, she could have at least sent her a card even if it said 'Glad I'm not there' it would be something. She finished her letter by saying everything at the gallery was fine, although David tended to panic a bit, he had been a good choice to look after things. With another plea for her to get in touch, or Belle would have to go over there, she signed her name with a flourish, sealed the envelope and went out to post the letter.

It was amazing how in just one month everything can change. Belle was enjoying her walk to the post box; the weather had changed dramatically, the evenings were lighter and the temperature had risen, it was warm enough to stroll without a jacket, having written to Anna, Belle suddenly felt the need for company, it hadn't occurred to her how much she missed her friend, man free for the moment, she called David on her mobile in the hope he would be free for dinner. She found him amusing and easy to talk to and, at that moment, she was desperately hoping he was available.

David was at a loose end and just wondering what to do with him-self that evening, when he picked up the phone. A smile spread across his face at the sound of Belle's voice.

"Of course," he said "dinner would be great", before suggesting they eat at the apartment and she could sample his amazing *pasta alla vongole*. Belle said she would bring the wine and some fresh bread, David went into the kitchen and started humming to him-self as he prepared the only meal he knew how to cook.

Belle looked at David standing in the doorway, he was grinning like a schoolboy, she thought to herself, *this is silly, its as though I'm going on a first date, but I've known him for ages,* then she thought, *no, I haven't, he was Anna's friend, if she hadn't gone we wouldn't have been thrown together in this way*. He reached out awkwardly and kissed her on the cheek leading her into the living room he relieved her of the wine and bread and excusing himself he went to the kitchen in search of the corkscrew. Once there he took a deep breath, *Oh god*, he thought, *I'm going to mess it up*. He realised as soon as he had seen her that he fancied her, he'd never been good at relationships, every one had ended in him being told he was a selfish git, but Belle had looked so fresh and lovely and her eyes, why hadn't he noticed how bright and blue those eyes were? Some artist he was; couldn't see what was under his nose. By the time David brought in the Italian wine, Belle had herself under control, she gave him an appreciative smile when he handed her the glass telling him she was starving. He visibly relaxed and said it was only a matter of minutes before they would eat.

Looking at the dining table, Belle thought he had gone to a lot of trouble for a casual dinner. The table which would normally seat eight, was laid up at one end; the two settings facing each other, a candle and flowers; beautiful vivid red tulips in centre position but not obscuring their view of each other. Belle wondered if David dined like this every evening. David, coming out from the kitchen caught her eye. He was carrying a large bowl of salad and a bowl of pasta, and putting both onto the table he beamed at her and said "*Voilà!*" She couldn't help but laugh. They spent the entire meal talking non-stop about their past lives telling each other intimate details of affairs that had gone wrong. Anna was the only other person Belle had told these things to and she could not believe how open she had been with David. He in turn had wanted her to know everything there was about himself, the reason being she could walk away when or if he ever plucked up the courage to tell her how he felt. *Hell!* He thought to himself as they cleared the table, *this dating business doesn't get any easier the older you get.*

For an artist, David was fairly conservative in his appearance. He was 41 years old and extremely attractive; blond, 5ft10 inches, very fit and because he enjoyed wine in the evening with his meal, he had decided exercise would be the only way to combat his excesses, he had bought himself a bicycle and each weekend would find him on the North Downs attempting to put right the wrongs of the previous week. They sat together comfortably on the sofa, David had opened another bottle of red, on impulse Belle leaned across and kissed him close to his mouth saying as she did so, "Thank you that meal was delicious."

He put his glass onto the coffee table and taking Belle's from her hand he kept his eyes locked with hers. Gently he brought her face up to meet his, their lips softly exploring each others, a small moan escaped from Belle and all of a sudden they were in a passionate embrace. Suddenly David stopped, stood up and reached for Belle's hand, she allowed herself to be led, not to Anna's room but to the guest bedroom. There David slowly began to undress her letting his hands slide slowly over her protruding nipples he unbuttoned her blouse releasing it from her shoulders his hands dropped down her back, the bra fell to the floor. David's eyes followed the curve of her small firm perky breasts, he kissed her eyes, nose, mouth and with his hand he explored the nape of her neck and very slowly brought it down to first one nipple then across to the other. Belle feeling the deep stirrings between her thighs wondered how long she could hold on before pulling him down on her. Sensing the arousal within her, David lay her on the bed, removing the long flowing skirt and silk panties his head immediately went down to explore and titillate her throbbing clitoris. She almost screamed her ecstasy; as her arousal reached its peak, not once but twice and she wanted him now. David allowed Belle to practically rip the clothes off his back, her hand guided him into her and he pulled her up to meet him, their bodies were bathed with sweat, their faces open in an expression of wanting, a deep moan escaped from David as he and Belle came together. Later as they lay in each others arms, comfortable, not needing to speak, just happy touching and kissing, similar thoughts were going through their minds. Belle had suddenly thought of Anna and how her departure had thrown them together, and David was quietly thanking Anna for asking him to look after the gallery, if it hadn't been for that, he probably would never have become so close to Belle. They instinctively moved closer together, Belle gently pushed David onto his back and sat astride him, he looked up at her feigning shock, "You insatiable woman," he said as he pulled Belle towards him. That night they both slept contented in each others arms, all thoughts of Anna and everyone else driven from their minds.

*

The case was as cold as Michael Foley's body lying in the morgue. No one had claimed him, Walters wondered to himself if Foley's boss would do the honours. *It might be just pushing things a bit too far, to expect Sir Geoffrey to bury the man he thinks is responsible for ruining the reputation of his firm, still, no harm in asking.*

Sir Geoffrey shook his head, "Inspector, are you joking?" They were in his office, Walters had said he thought it might be a bit much to ask; but the body needed to be buried and the inspector could only think of one person to approach. Sir Geoffrey could not believe what was being asked of him, he had asked the inspector himself to investigate Foley's behaviour and now he was being asked to bury the man? "For God's sake; the whole idea is ridiculous!"

Walters put his hand up to stop Sir Geoffrey's tirade, he said "I'm sorry Sir; but it was only a suggestion, all I ask is that you think about it." At the back of his mind was the thought, *and it would save me even more paperwork*. Two days later, after speaking to his partners Sir Geoffrey Tyne telephoned Walters and informed him of his decision to assume responsibility for the cremation of Mr Michael Foley.

Seven weeks after he had been murdered, Michael Foley was cremated with very little ceremony and no friends or family to say goodbye. The few who turned up at the small crematorium just outside London were, in the main, colleagues or police officers. Walters couldn't help himself feeling a twinge of sadness; no one should live for 35 years and die without at least having one friend to mourn him. After the coffin had disappeared behind the curtain, Walters slipped from his position at the back of the small chapel, waiting outside, he watched as the dozen so-called mourners emerged. When Sir Geoffrey finally appeared, Inspector Walters strode toward him, looking at his face he could see how tense the man was, shaking his hand, Walters thanked Sir Geoffrey for doing the honours; Sir Geoffrey's reply was that he couldn't very well leave the man lying in a freezer, and he asked the inspector if any leads had been discovered about who might have killed him. Inspector Walters knew Sammy had found evidence about Foley's lifestyle and his dealings with certain high-ranking people, but at the moment things were still being kept quiet, more needed to be known before any of these men could be approached; shaking his head he told Sir Geoffrey nothing new had come to light.

The inspector didn't really wish to take his leave but after the rows with his wife he knew she would go without him so, Sergeant Clarke was being left to try and sort out the backlog of paperwork, and he was welcome to it! The fraud squad had at least three weeks more to prepare some sort of case before they could proceed any further. Walters and his wife were due to fly into Malaga airport the day after Foley's funeral.

Maro

On arriving at Malaga, the Walters' found a taxi waiting to ferry them to the apartment that Mrs Walters had booked. The inspector had left all the details of the holiday to his wife and was happy for once to be guided by her, after all if the holiday was a disaster it would be her fault, *but*, he thought to himself as the driver led them to the car, *so far so good*; the plane had actually been on time and now someone was greeting them, all be it in a language he couldn't understand, and taking them straight to where they were going to stay for the next fortnight. Had Walters known what the journey would be like, he doubted if he would have got into the cab. Never in his life had he experienced a car ride like that; his whole body was taut from the tension of it, once they had left the airport the driver not only spoke but drove at 100 miles per hour. Walters' wife kept looking at him with an expression of rising panic, but Walters returned her stare with a sick nonchalant smile, never having been to the Spanish mainland before he tried to concentrate by looking out on the vast mountain scenery that was flashing past. The journey, normally one that took an hour, was over in 40 minutes. Mrs Walters was as white as a sheet when the driver pulled up outside the large, white block of concrete, and Walters himself, feeling slightly queasy, climbed out of the car and tentatively held on to the door, not wishing his wife to see how much his legs were shaking. The driver having been paid his fare, said to them in broken English that when their holiday was finished he would be very pleased to return them to the airport; and pushed his card into Walters hand, the inspector said nothing, he had yet to find his voice; waving the driver off they both stood very still taking in great gulps of air. Taking control, Mrs Walters extracted the keys of the apartment from her handbag and instructed her husband to follow her. Going up in the lift to the sixth floor, Walters thought the inside of the building seemed a trifle more inviting than its exterior. Leaving the elevator they walked down a long, narrow, marbled corridor until they reached the door facing them. Inserting the key into the lock Mrs Walters turned to her husband with a smile, she knew what the interior was like because she had seen photographs her husband was in for a pleasant surprise, but all Walters was thinking at that moment was he wanted to get rid of these cases and have a pint of beer; his eyes almost popped out of his head as he surveyed the huge sitting/dining room, it was like something out of one of those home and garden magazines his wife was always buying. The large terrace stretched all the way from the bedroom to the living area, and although there was only one bedroom it seemed massive in comparison to theirs at home. Perhaps this holiday wasn't going to be too bad after all; he went up to his wife who was standing on the terrace looking out to sea and gave her a cuddle, she giggled like a schoolgirl and told him there were some beers in the fridge; they both needed a drink after that taxi ride.

The first week in May was a beautiful time to visit Spain, the weather was warming up nicely and it wasn't too busy in the restaurants and bars. Inspector Walters was amazed at the itinerary his wife had put together; normally all she wanted to do was lay on the beach and read but she had made plans for a different excursion almost every day, although for the first few days she had insisted he just relax and become acclimatised; she wanted him to slow down, and by the third day he was acting like one of the locals. The gentle pace calmed him and although he caught himself wondering on occasion how 'Nobby' was getting on, he had started to enjoy just being with his wife. Hiring a car, they visited the Alhambra at Granada, leaving Torrox at the unearthly hour of 8am, and heading east. The road followed the shoreline for several kilometres, with high cliffs to the left and the vast expanse of sea, only yards away, to the right of them.

They climbed a small hill and descended into the fertile delta of the Rio Chillar, with the fishing town of Nerja in the distance. Driving through the sleeping town, past the bus and taxi ranks, Tim and Marie saw little signs of life, and they both agreed it was the best time to be on the road. There was even less traffic as they headed towards the village of Maro. Marie mentioned to her husband this was the site of the famous Nerja caves and they would be visiting them in a few days. Just before reaching the village they passed a disused but dignified sugar factory and an extremely old looking aqueduct. The beautifully maintained coast road afforded spectacular views of the numerous small beaches and coves that scattered the coastline.

Twinkling like sparkling jewels the sun danced on the sea, as it peaked over the distant mountains its glow created a golden light on the Martello towers that stood to attention on the most prominent points, a reminder of an era when this magnificent coast was the domain of ferocious pirates. Having driven up the Cerro Gordo, Marie begged Tim to stop; grabbing the camera from the glove compartment she jumped out of the car before Tim had managed to turn off the ignition.

"This place is heaven!" Marie said; they were standing in front of The Mirador Restaurant, and to the right of them the views were of Nerja and beyond, Torrox. As his wife started taking photographs, Tim looked over to the left and down at the beautiful horseshoe bay of La Herradura. It was all stunning, but Tim knew if they were ever to reach Granada, the stops would need to be kept to a minimum, so with this in mind he called his excited wife back to the car. Looking at her guide book, Marie informed her husband that this area was called the Costa Tropical, and they had been in the province of Granada for the past 5km, Tim, with a smile playing at his lips, realised the whole drive would be like a guided tour with his wife dropping snippets from the book during their journey.

They continued on and after 15 minutes they arrived at Solobrena, a town dominated by its medieval castle. Reading again from the guide, Marie said, "Now we are in the delta of the Rio Guadalfeo, where over hundreds of years, harnessing the water spilling down from the Alpujaras and the Sierra Navada made this area a prosperous market garden."

Finally they turned in-land and as they gently climbed, following the course of the Guadalfeo River, the high peaks of the Sierra Navada appeared, and even though it was early May the majestic mountains still had a thick covering of snow. The road carried on, past white villages that looked very precariously perched on lumps of rock. Higher and higher they climbed until suddenly they reached a plateau; Marie was acting the tour guide again, "Just up ahead is the Puerto del Suspiro del Moro,"

Tim burst out laughing, "What?" Marie looked at him. "I'm sorry love but suddenly you have developed a Spanish accent."

"Well I am only trying to pronounce the names properly!" she said, looking peeved.

"No you carry on; I'm really enjoying listening to the history," she gave him another of her looks and he coaxed her with another "please?"

"OK, Puerto del Suspiro del Moro in English it means 'The Pass of the Sighing Moor', and was named after the last Moorish ruler of Granada, and as he was retreating from the armies of Isabel and Ferdinand, he looked back at his beloved city and the Alhambra. He had tears in his eyes; his mother who was beside him said; 'Why do you weep like a woman for what you could not fight for as a man?'"

"You wouldn't have wanted to get on the wrong side of her!" Tim said.

Stopping the car they saw Granada in the distance: the magnificent fortress stood bathed in golden sunshine, "No wonder the moors had ruled for over 700 years" Walters mused; the passage from the sea over the mountain terrain would put most but the foolhardy off ever getting this far. It was just approaching 11am and he and his wife decided to have coffee in town before walking up to the Alhambra. Later, speaking to Marie he found the adjectives he chose to describe what they had seen seemed inadequate; they had taken the main road back from Granada, and although they had had a long day they were far from tired. Mrs Walters suggested they stop at a little village just along the coast road from where they were staying, have some dinner and stretch their legs. When Walters drove around the place it looked dead and he said so to his wife, but just as he was deciding to drive straight through Mrs Walters told him to stop. He parked the car in front of the bar. It had a long, wide veranda with about half a dozen tables and chairs, two of which were occupied, at one table sat three elderly Spanish men, sipping cervasas and eating tapas, at the other sat a tall, slim woman with the most beautiful mane of auburn hair, Walters thought to himself, *if she weren't so skinny she would be beautiful*. Anna had been watching the couple alight from their car, as they came closer she surmised they were English, from their certain way of looking around finding their bearings. Her eyes were failing and although the sun was just setting she realised they were not as old as she first thought. They seated themselves at a table adjacent to hers.

Listening to their conversation she gleaned they had been to Granada. Inspector Walters, glancing over at Anna's table saw a small smile play about her lips. He knew that she was listening them so when the waiter arrived to take their order, he deliberately made out he couldn't understand, and to his wife's bemusement, asked Anna is she could help in the translation. Her voice when she spoke had a rasping sound to it, and when in mid-sentence she would stop to catch her breath Inspector Walters realised this woman was very ill and felt ashamed he had disturbed her but Anna didn't mind, she found the small diversion amusing. The couple introduced themselves as Tim and Marie, Anna asked where they were staying and if they were enjoying their holiday. Tim and Marie were animated about the places they had been, the scenery and the people; Inspector Walters and his wife had fallen in love with Spain. They described how they had taken the route they had taken and the wonderful scenery; Anna was fascinated not by the couple but by their description of their journey. Her attention span at this time was very short and she had been speaking with the couple for over half an hour, Walters was just describing the Generalife gardens when an old man arrived and spoke to Anna. Vincente asked Anna if she was ready to go home, in Spanish she told him to wait in the bar and have a drink, she would call him when she was ready if he didn't mind, Vincente was only too pleased, Mia hadn't allowed him out for almost four days because Miss Anna had been so poorly, and she was frightened of being alone in case anything happened. Going into the bar, Vincente greeted Alberto the owner with a nod; they had known each other all their lives but as in most small villages acted very stand-offish toward each other.

Walters had watched the exchange between these two totally different people and he had seen the affection in both their eyes, the old man with his black beret firmly perched above his weather-beaten face, a face that looked as though it could tell a thousand stories, but also a face that was true and would give nothing away. The waiter had brought their food and Anna had turned away to sip her iced water, why was it that British people felt obtrusive when other people were eating?

Walters asked Anna if she would join him and his wife in a drink and smiling, Anna said although she would love a wine and it probably would be cheaper, water was the only drink she was able to have at the moment due to a small medical problem. Walters said it didn't matter, he didn't mind paying extra for the ice and lemon.

Watching from inside the bar, Vincente's protective gaze was veering from Anna to the couple at the adjoining table, the couple were unknown to him but he was aware of how tourists would pop into local bars and just strike up conversations with the people at the next table, he was also aware of how Miss Anna was feeling and he should be insisting on her going home. Just as he had decided to go, Anna raised her hand very slightly, he was immediately by her side and she told him she had invited Tim and Maria back for coffee.

Both Walters and his wife were surprised that this frail, rasping woman had invited them to her home; whereas Walters was more than willing, his wife thought it was all very well talking to someone in a bar but going back to their home was a different matter, it could prove very embarrassing. Vincente helped Anna out of the chair, Mrs Walters looked at her husband, she felt very awkward, he shrugged his shoulders, this woman intrigued him, and what the hell, she wanted them to go and have a coffee so why not?

They walked the 150 metres to her villa very slowly. Anna stopped every so often and catching her breath, would make a comment about the view over the sea or how the lights over Nerja seemed so bright, had they been to the town yet? When answering 'no'; she said they should as it was such a wonderful town. Her attitude was wistful as though all she wanted to do was to go there.

Eventually they reached double black iron gates, Vincente opened it with a key, and inspector Walters could hear a dog barking somewhere deep in the undergrowth of what seemed to be an enormous garden. They walked down a long path toward a bright porch light and eventually reached double doors, which were opened by a small, dark, Spanish woman.

Her glance towards Anna was one of concern which turned to amazement on seeing the Walters standing behind her. Anna spoke only Spanish to the two old people and she asked Mia to bring coffee and Brandy for her guests, they would sit out on the terrace.

As Mia left, Anna turned to the Walters and guided them toward the living room and out to the terrace. Marie Walters' eyes were almost popping out of her head, she had thought the apartment they were staying in was luxurious, but this woman's home was like something out of a dream. Inspector Walters eyes were transfixed by the paintings adorning the walls turning at the sound of Anna's voice he apologised and said he had never seen a more beautiful setting for works of art than this. Anna glowed and explained that until recently she had been involved with the art world but illness had forced her to take early retirement, the Walters didn't wish to seem nosey and did not ask about her illness, they just nodded and Anna changed the subject, asking what their plans for the rest of their holiday were. Mrs Walters said they would be visiting the caves above Maro the following day and as they only had four days left had hoped to go to Competa on one of them.

Anna suggested they drive to Competa the following morning and even gave them the name of a good restaurant to stop at for lunch on the way back. Walters was quite surprised until Anna said if they went to the caves in two day's time she would like them to join her for lunch. Mia had brought the coffee and brandy, a light sea breeze was caressing their skins and with the smell of jasmine mingled with the aroma of rich coffee, Marie and Tim looked at each other for confirmation and both said at the same time they would love to come for lunch.

Laughing at their reaction, Anna said "Great that's settled!" Although it was barely 10pm the Walters did not wish to overstay their welcome, their hostess seemed to be tiring, so making the excuse that it had been a long day, they shook Anna's hand when she led them through the atrium towards the double doors. Vincente was waiting to lead them along the path, opening the gates he raised his hat and bid them *adiós*, thanking him in Spanish the Walters slowly walked back to their car; for them both the day had been a moving experience, seeing the Alhambra and Granada and meeting Anna a very rare person indeed.

Later, sitting on their own terrace, Tim and Marie retraced the day, culminating in their encounter with Anna. "I must say I found it extraordinary," Marie mused, "I mean, you don't normally end up in people's homes after just meeting in a bar, do you?"

Tim looked across and said, "You are glad we did though; you know you will be telling all your mates about the villa and Anna for weeks to come." He was also thinking of the villa, or more precisely, what was hanging on the villa walls.

The paintings, at least three of them were by the same artists that hung in Foley's apartment, Tim Walters did not believe in coincidence and pondered the idea of phoning Nobby Clark.

London

Sergeant Clarke had been able to concentrate on the backlog of paperwork his boss had left, and after the first week he was able to get back to the telephone numbers on the Foley list, he decided to go back to the gallery and find out if the owner had returned.

The weather was still fairly warm but continuous rain was making everyone feel miserable. Telephoning the gallery, Sergeant Clarke received no answer, which he thought unusual; the time was only 12.30 surely they didn't lunch this early; he would try again this afternoon. At that moment David had just left the premises, he was meeting Belle for lunch at Chelsea Harbour. Everything in David and Belle's garden was rosy, life, for them both seemed perfect. The love they had found together had grown in intensity over the last few weeks and they had barely been apart. Belle was due to go abroad at the end of the month and she would be away for at least six weeks, David didn't want her to go but knew better than to make his feelings known. He wanted nothing to ruin this relationship, Belle for her part had never felt happier; she couldn't believe the depth of her feelings for David. What had surprised her most was the fact of her giving in totally to those feelings. They had three short weeks before Belle's trip, she didn't want to leave him but her work was suffering and she felt that the break might just put her feet back on the ground.

Jumping out of the taxi, Belle ran up the steps to the Chinese restaurant and almost knocked David over with her enthusiastic hug. He laughed and wiped the rain droplet from her forehead. They were like two young lovers as they entered the restaurant hand in hand. Belle had re-read the letters she had received from Anna, and as she said to David, had found them very strange; her writing seemed scratchy and erratic and although she said she was having a great time and the peace and quiet was doing her the power of good, the rest of her letter was vague and rambling, it just wasn't her usual style. David said she may have written it in a rush, and if she said she was fine there was no need to worry, but secretly what perturbed him was that she hadn't mentioned the gallery, the place had been her life and not one line had she written as to how David was coping, he had to admit it was strange. He wasn't surprised when Belle said she was going to make a detour down to Spain when she had completed her buying trip, it would mean they would be separated for an extra week but she really needed to see Anna for herself and make sure everything was alright. At that moment Belle decided to tell David everything she knew about Michael Foley. At first she could barely say his name, looking down at the food on the table, her appetite disappeared. David poured wine into her glass and held her hand. Slowly she relaxed.

"It was almost five years ago" Belle said; her eyes took on a faraway look as she remembered Anna's beaming smile, describing how Michael, after browsing around the gallery had approached her, "She told me, 'His eyes just bored through me, and before I knew it he had purchased a painting and we were out of the gallery and having lunch at the local wine bar.' She was so happy. He told her he was in Hedge Funds, Anna hadn't a clue what that was, so he explained it in what he called 'simple' terms:

"'As a Hedge manager, I use quite sophisticated derivatives, such as futures contracts, options and puts, the products all do two things; they use small amounts of money or leverage and promise large amounts of stock or commodities, but we have to deliver this stock at a certain time; so I need to be very sure of the market to make it work.'

"Of course," Belle said, "when he said 'derivatives', Anna stopped listening and stared into his eyes, nodding every few minutes just to make out she was interested, it was the first and last time they spoke of his work.

"He told her his parents had died when he was young; and that is probably what sealed it for Anna; that one common fact; she automatically assumed he felt the same as she did about losing her mother and father. I didn't actually meet him until about the fourth week, and when I did I couldn't understand why she was so besotted; yes, he was tall, dark and from a distance, attractive, but I found him cold and when we spoke the conversation was stilted. When Anna suggested we all go down to the local pub; Michael looked petulant, and said 'I have already booked a table in the west end.' I was being dismissed and Anna didn't even realise what was going on.

After that introduction, I made sure I met Anna when she was on her own and we rarely spoke of Michael if I could help it. Then, it must have been about five months later Anna called me. She sounded really upset; just as I arrived at the apartment Foley swung the door open, he had a face like thunder, he literally barged into me. I don't think I have ever seen that much hatred in a person's face before.

I found Anna in her bedroom, she was very pale and shaking, so I put her to bed and made some tea. As we drank it Anna told me what had happened the previous night.

They had a routine, Michael could apparently only see her two nights during the week and on Sundays, I could never understand why she thought that was normal. Anyway, one of the artists Anna exhibited had delivered some new canvases, so, knowing what Michael liked; she decided to take one over to his apartment after closing the gallery that evening, unable to get him on his mobile she decided to surprise him.

When she arrived there was no answer to her ring on the doorbell, and letting herself in with the key he had given her a month earlier she propped the painting against the wall in the living room. Everything was quiet and as she was debating whether to leave a note or not, there was a sound; it came from the direction of the bedroom. Smiling as she went to check it out she realised Michael must have been in the shower. That smile froze on Anna's face when she opened the bedroom door, she took in the tableau on the bed, and bile rose up into her throat; her head swam with the confusion of it all. Foley had his back to her, under him was what looked like a child, and watching them, a skinny, naked youth. Three sets of eyes turned as though in slow motion to look at Anna. When he saw her watching, a smile appeared on his lips, and Foley said to her, 'Why don't you come and join us?'

"Not stopping to retrieve the painting, Anna blindly found her way outside, and taking in great gulps of air managed to find a taxi to take her home."

David was holding her hand tightly, Belle tried to stop the tears falling but they escaped. Pulling herself together, she said, "The bastard had the gall to go to Anna's the next day with the painting! He said it was crap, and she obviously had no idea what he liked; *he* would no longer be seeing her, and would like his keys back, nothing was mentioned about the young boys. Anna told me she went to her purse, retrieved the keys and walked to the door. Holding the keys up with the door open, she waited;

Foley walked slowly toward her with a look of pity in his eyes, and that's what did it."

"What?" David was confused.

Belle lifted her smiling face to him and said, "She kneed him in the balls and threw him down the stairs, it's a wonder he didn't break his neck! Honestly, even though she was in such a state I couldn't help laughing, and Anna did too for a minute, but it was all so raw for her.

"I stayed for two days, and all she could talk about was the sight that met her when she opened that bedroom door, it seemed to be emblazoned on her brain. She went to Spain for a couple of months, and there was a semblance of her former self when she returned."

It was David's turn to be shocked "Bloody hell! Why did she not report him to the police about the boys?"

"We talked it over, but she had no idea what age they were, only that fact that they looked so young."

*

Sergeant Clarke was waiting outside the gallery when David returned from lunch. David didn't recognise the police officer at first, when he had re-introduced himself, David showed him into the back office, seating himself he explained the owner was not expected to return for at least another three months. The sergeant told him that he was investigating a murder and he needed to get in touch with the owner, an address or telephone number would help. David only had the address of her villa, as she was not on the phone, so he gave the sergeant her name and address and told him Anna was there for recuperation; she had been ill; couldn't the police wait until she had fully recovered? Surely anything she had to tell them could wait. Later on the sergeant and David would wonder if it would have made any difference had the police written to Anna. Had Sergeant Clarke known the Spanish coastline at all, he would have realised his boss was holidaying only 5 miles from Anna's villa.

The case of finding those responsible behind Michael Foley's insider dealings had come to a standstill. Sammy had interviewed the list of names and apart from one person, who he thought he had rattled sufficiently, had managed to get nowhere. He knew they had been warned off but could not find out by whom. The evidence collected showed

Foley could not have engineered the fraud solely he must have had strong backing.

Sir Geoffrey Tyne was unable to control his anger when Sammy told him the case would have to be put on the backburner, unless someone showed their hand, and he didn't expect that to happen. Word had reached the trading rooms of the rumours about Tyne, Wheeler and Munch, the young traders who had come up on Foley's shirt tails were keeping a low profile, the shock of finding out the man they all wanted to emulate had been involved in dirty dealings and was probably killed because of it, left a bad smell around the office, self preservation had become the name of the game.

Sir Geoffrey knew that someone close to the top had helped Michael Foley with his dealings, someone else had lined their pockets with millions which should have been his firm's and they were not going to get away with it no matter what the fraud squad thought.

Sir Geoffrey was almost apoplectic with rage, Martin Weller was on the receiving end and his own face was white with anger, he would have loved to walk out of the office but couldn't bring himself to move as Sir Geoffrey's tirade grew.

What was coming out was the fact that Sir Geoffrey had remembered he was responsible for introducing Foley and not only that, it was his responsibility to have overseen his dealings. Weller tried to respond but couldn't get a word in edgeways.

Normally, Weller would not have taken any of the abuse being thrown at him, but it was in his own best interest at the moment to keep quiet and take whatever Sir Geoffrey felt like dishing out. He needed to know everything that the police had told his partner and the only way, unfortunately, was to be his battering ram for the moment. So far as he could make out, nothing new had developed.

Sitting alone afterwards, Sir Geoffrey frowned at the thought of Weller's reaction; it had been so unlike him to sit and take what amounted to verbal abuse. In fact, looking back over the past few weeks Weller's behaviour had been cagey. He had always thought the man standoffish and pompous but of late his attitude had become almost humble, and when someone changes to that extent it's because they have done something. If it was what he thought it was, no amount of humble behaviour would save him.

Flicking through his personal phone book, Sir Geoffrey punched the outside line and dialled the number, if the police couldn't get anywhere perhaps a little shove in the right direction would help.

The man Sir Geoffrey met at the sandwich bar in Duke Street, looked insignificant, which only added to his suitability for the job in hand. As a private investigator Stubbs was one of the best in London; Sir Geoffrey had used his services only once before and had been impressed by his thoroughness and discretion.

On receiving his brief, Stubbs nodded and assured Sir Geoffrey he would get back to him as soon as possible; Stubbs knew the police could not use the resources he was privy to, he reckoned it would be perhaps one week or 10 days before there would be any results. Sir Geoffrey Tyne was in for the shock of his life.

Maro

Two days after their trip to Granada, Inspector Walters awoke feeling very hungover. The previous day's trip into the mountains with its combination of soaring temperatures and Malaga wine had taken its toll and his wife looked at him with a smug grin on her face. Their arrangement had been that he would drive up the mountain to Competa and she would drive back. She had not minded until they had almost reached the village; she hadn't realised how winding and narrow the road would be. Marie Walters had never been so sober in her life, but her husband had made up for the two of them, drinking beer before lunch, and wine during lunch and Malaga wine after lunch.

He had not looked this bad for a long time, it was a shame they had agreed to go to Anna's that afternoon, the poor man should really have stayed in bed; but a promise was a promise and Marie was looking forward to seeing Anna and her gorgeous home again. She made her husband drink strong, sweet, black coffee in the hope he might look human by lunchtime and went to get ready.

Visiting the caves seemed to put a bit of life back into Tim Walters, it was another of those moments that would be indelibly printed in his memory. On entering the caves what hit them at first was the cold air followed by almost blackness.

Adjusting their eyes they started to descend a steep wooden staircase. Before reaching the midway point a flash of light caught them with a surprised grimace on their faces, later they would discover a photo could be purchased of their visit. Again they had to adjust their eyes, and coming to a long, wooden bridge they stopped to survey the most amazing stalactites and stalagmites to be uncovered.

Underneath the bridge they were standing on a stage had been set, apparently for a short summer season of ballet and concerts due to take place the following month. Emerging from the coolness of the cave into the blazing midday sun they did what every other tourist had done before them and went to get their photograph.

A revived Tim Walters climbed into the hire car, and laughing with his wife at the expression they both displayed in the photo, slowly drove down the hill into the town of Maro.

It was an hour before they were due at Anna's for lunch so they decided to have a coffee at the bar where they had met her. Walters sat close to his wife he played with her hand, entwining his fingers with hers. They had always been very close and she could read him like a book, he wasn't a man that wore his heart on his sleeve, but when something moved him, his tears were clearly visible to her.

Sitting there he tried to find the words to thank her for giving him the most wonderful holiday he had ever experienced, she looked up at him with raised eyebrows as he planted a kiss on her lips. Marie understood what he was trying to convey to her and touched his face; she suggested a walk around the village.

They strolled up the slight incline until they reached the hotel at the entrance to Maro, and taking a right turn walked downward past the tomato factory. It was just coming up to 1.30pm when they came across the church square, looking at it from a different angle, Walters realised they were almost upon Anna's villa. Although he and his wife had discussed the situation he still felt it was an intrusion. Standing outside the gates, they waited for a response to their buzzing, none was forthcoming.

Glancing around Marie Walters noticed a few people at the bar on the corner looking in their direction, *probably locals being nosey* she thought, Inspector Walters buzzed again, he didn't think Anna was the type of person to invite people to lunch and then renegade on it.

They heard movement behind the gates and turning together looked expectantly as they opened, beside Vincente stood a man dressed formally in a dark suit. The smiles the Walters had planted on their faces faded at the expressions of both men, Vincente explained to the doctor who the two people were and the doctor in turn spoke to them in English; unfortunately Anna was very ill and unable to receive visitors at the moment perhaps in a few days she may feel able to cope but he was sorry, no visitors were allowed at present. Being polite British people they asked Vincente to give Anna their best wishes and hoped she would have a speedy recovery but unfortunately they had to return to England in two days. They had enjoyed their trip so much that when they returned, hopefully, they would be able to meet with Anna again.

Vincente, his eyes filled with tears, could only nod his head, he shook their hands and raised his beret, the last glimpse they had was of an old weather-beaten man, who, if possible, had aged another 10 years in only two days.

The doctor was walking to his car and on impulse Walters left his wife and walked quickly over to him, touching his arm he apologised for intruding and asked if the doctor could give him any idea when Anna might recover. The doctor stared into his eyes, and after a moment's hesitation he decided to tell this total stranger straight that no, she would never recover; at best she had two weeks to live at worst four weeks; in his opinion, the woman had fought for too long already.

Although Tim Walters had known somewhere in the back of his mind that Anna was dying, somehow the doctors stark words were a shock to him, thanking the doctor, (although a 'thank you' seemed stupid under the circumstances), he turned on his heel and walked stiffly back to his wife.

They drove to Nerja, Marie could hardly bear the silence, but Tim had that closed look which said 'I'll talk about it in my own good time'. Walking down Pintada the main street, they strolled to the end of the Balcon. Tim Walters looked at his wife, he didn't understand why, but tears were pricking his eyes, taking her hands in his he told her what the doctor had said, they had only spent four hours in Anna's life, but somehow the fact they would no longer see her or be able to say how sorry they were made them feel drained, it was all so desperately sad. They stood for a few moments looking out at the calm sea with their arms around each other, thinking, a young life was about to end; and they felt impotent.

When Mia entered Anna's bedroom, she watched as the girl she thought of as a daughter slept, the sun had just reached the top of her pillow and it shone on her beautiful hair creating a golden halo. Anna's face in repose did not look tranquil, the pain she had suffered over the past months showed in every line.

Mia almost dropped the flowers she was carrying, moving closer to the bed Anna looked dead, tentatively, she approached her, laying the flowers on the table she gently put her hand on Anna's cheek, a small movement from the bed made Mia exhale with relief. As her eyes tried to focus,

Anna could see Mia's shadow, the old woman started speaking in rapid Spanish, something about the English couple.

After a few minutes she understood, the couple she had met had sent her flowers and there was a note but Mia couldn't read it. When the doctor arrived he read it for her, it said 'Sorry we couldn't make if for lunch; it was wonderful to have met you, we shall definitely return to Spain, hope you feel better soon; god bless and good luck, Tim and Marie.'

To Mia it was a relief to have the live-in nurse; having to wash and change Anna every few hours had really worn her down. When speaking to Vincente the previous evening, they discussed the fact that Anna would have no-one but themselves at the end; while Mia thought it a terrible thing, Vincente said it was what she wanted; they argued into the night, the month before, Anna had written a letter and told Vincente to post it on her death; but looking at it, Vincente decided perhaps this was the time; before it was too late.

London

Belle was up to her eyes in work, trying to sort out her timetable for the buying trip and see as much of David as she could was exhausting, she was rushing out the door to go to work when she collided with the postman he handed her the mail. A Spanish stamp caught her eye. Belle put the rest of the post on the hall table and Anna's letter into her bag, she would read it later, the thought of a nice chatty letter from Anna put a smile on her face; it was about the only thing that could first thing in the morning.

*

Sergeant Clarke looked up from behind his boss's desk to find him standing in the doorway, he rose and walked towards Inspector Walters, he shook his hand. Feeling slightly embarrassed Walters put a brusque tone to his voice and asked his sergeant if anything had emerged in the Foley case, when the reply was negative he shook his head, he had hoped Sammy would come up with something. The Sergeant tentatively asked if he had a good holiday, into Walters' head an image of Anna appeared but looking at Nobby Clarke he smiled and said it was the best holiday he had ever had.

As Inspector Walters was looking at the updated report on Michael Foley?, he caught sight of a familiar name and address, he could not believe it, what on earth was this person doing in connection with Foley.

At exactly the same moment Walters was puzzling on his find, Belle was reading Anna's letter, and it was a matter of moments before she was groping blindly for the telephone. David answered on the third ring, Belle was almost incoherent from sobbing; trying to calm her down all he could understand was that she had read a letter from Anna. He told her to get a cab and come over to the gallery straight away.

Sitting in the black cab, Belle could barely contain the shaking that had convulsed her body. David paid the driver and helped Belle into the shop. Locking the door behind them, he almost had to lift her into the office. Belle was as white as a sheet as she handed David the letter.

'*My dearest Belle,*' Anna had written.

'*I am deeply sorry I have to write this letter; that I couldn't be truthful with you before I left; but darling Belle, I wanted to try and spare you as much pain as possible.*

As you know I haven't been very well recently, in actual fact I've been ill for the past four years. There is no simple way of telling you; by the time you read this, I will have died. I have asked Vincente to post this letter after my death, I know this will hurt you very much, please forgive me but knowing the care and attention I need in the final months I couldn't put you through that. Also, by the time the end comes the illness will have brought on blindness and dementia and I couldn't allow you, my only true friend to go through that.

I want you to remember me as I truly was, not the wreck I am becoming. Belle, I have HIV, and I was infected by Michael Foley. I have thought about everything that happened and although Michael may have infected me the blame can only lie at my own door. I knew at the time what I was doing, you know how madly in love I was with Michael, at the beginning I thought he loved me, but we both know how it ended.

Unfortunately I came away with more than I had bargained for. And I didn't know where to turn, I did think of telling you, often, but it did not seem right to give you that burden. I know you will say I was wrong but please do your best to understand it from my point of view.

Belle you are my best friend, please believe I have kept you away for all the right reasons, in the end I may be wrong but I never wanted to hurt you or anyone else. Who was it said 'Death isn't for the feint hearted', what a load of shit, how many people who know they are going to die, stand back and take it on the chin? They don't; they fight tooth and nail, kicking and screaming to the end. Death happens to everyone and the lucky ones don't know anything about it, I just wish I were one of them. '

I want to live so much. I realise this sounds melodramatic and I can imagine your face as you read these lines Belle, I can only say again 'I hope you forgive me.'

Remember when we were teenagers, how we would save our lunch money for months and then spend a Saturday walking around London, always ending up at Charlotte Street for afternoon tea, we thought we were so grown up. Then when we really could afford it we would make it our monthly outing, come rain or shine.

If good memories go with you, I shall have an abundance; with you at the core. I'm glad you and David have started to see each other, please be happy and give my love to him. You will find out soon that the business, flat and house in Spain are yours, I would only ask that you keep on Mia and Vincente because they have shown me love and great care in these last months.

There is so much to be said but I am emotionally and physically drained. All I ask is that you keep our good memories in your heart and take them out now and again for a laugh, because we had lots of those.

I love you Belle, I'm sorry I had to tell you everything this way.

Please forgive me;

with my love,

forever yours,

Anna

Practically before he had finished the letter David was on the phone booking two tickets to Malaga. The next flight was in four hours, enough time for them to pick up their passports and pack a few things. They were at Heathrow with 30 minutes to spare. Just as Belle and David were landing at Malaga, Inspector Walters was ringing on the door at the gallery, to no avail.

Belle and David arrived at 10.30pm, buzzing the gate they waited. It was 10 minutes before Vincente answered. He looked at them; Belle wondered if he would remember her since she hadn't been there for over two years but as recognition dawned on him, Vincente opened the gates and almost fell upon her, speaking half in English and half Spanish; he cried out how Miss Anna was still alive but very bad.

Belle and David couldn't believe it! They had expected her to be dead and buried. Almost running to her bedroom, Belle stopped outside the door, catching her breath. She was silently praying Anna would know her.

Slowly opening the door, her first impression was of the two women sitting just to the right of the bed, they both looked toward her, Mia almost smiled, but her sadness ran too deep. The bedroom was lit only by the moon.

Mia rose from her chair and reached for Belle's hand. She guided her toward the bed, looking at Mia, Belle asked if they could have a light on, Anna was in a deep sleep, her best friend felt as though someone had kicked her in the stomach; Belle couldn't catch her breath. On the bed lay a skeleton, the hair was Anna's but this old woman was not Anna.

Belle had to remember how she described the illness in her letter, she had to remember how much she wanted to be here; now that she was, she needed to be strong. Moving closer she bent over and kissed Anna on the forehead, with her hand she stroked her friend's hair. *Please God*, she thought, *let her wake in the morning and know me*.

Mia showed them to the guest room, where they left their bags on the bed and went directly to the living area. Vincente and Mia stood by the door; Belle asked them to please sit down.

Although she only had a smattering of Spanish, Belle was able to discover what Anna's last months had been like, she also found out that it was Mia's nagging at Vincente which prompted him to send the letter before he was supposed to; which she told them she would be eternally grateful for.

Mia said there would be no point their staying up all night. Anna was comfortable and would sleep all night because of the medication; she would go to the kitchen and make them something to eat. Belle thought if she saw food she would throw up but Mia was determined.

When they left the room, David went over to Belle, he had kept fairly silent all the time they had been there, putting his arms round her he could feel the release of tension which had gripped her body all day. They went out onto the terrace and standing there, they breathed in the Mediterranean air, it seemed all the more unbelievable that Anna was lying in a room just below them, dying. It was the guilt Belle couldn't handle, she was here fit and healthy and in love, her friend was here dying. Belle suddenly broke down, the sobs racking her body. David wanted to break down also, but felt he couldn't. Mia found them clutching each other when she returned; she had been grieving for so long, she felt immune to the grief in others.

They sat for a long time on the terrace, Mia had brought brandy and coffee and David insisted Belle should drink it. He mind felt as if an explosion had detonated in it. She wanted to scream at the top of her voice. David kept his own council; the shock of the past twelve hours had left him feeling numb. Looking at Belle's stricken face, all he wished he could do was to hold her and say it was all a bad dream, it would pass but it wouldn't and this was life at its rawest and most cruel. They needed sleep and David told Belle if she were to be of any use to Anna in the morning she had better go to bed, he would be along soon.

Left alone, David was able to take in his surroundings for the first time. He stood by the terrace railing and looked out at the ebony night, the half moon through a shimmering light on to the sea below; it felt as if time had stood still. Turning, David looked into the living room, even as an artist he could not have envisaged more beautiful surroundings for the magnificent works Anna had collected for her own enjoyment. Walking about the room he looked at each painting in turn, it dawned on him she would never again be able to see these paintings, it was then David cried.

At six the next morning, Mia brought tea to Belle and David's room, leaving it on the coffee table by the window she told Belle; Anna had had a peaceful night, she had not yet awakened. David poured the tea, handing the cup to Belle; he was relieved to see she had stopped shaking and looked a lot calmer. He had not yet seen Anna, not wishing to intrude; he felt it would be better to wait until after Belle had spoken to her. She was grateful for David's presence, if it were not for him she didn't think she could cope.

Entering Anna's bedroom, more with trepidation at the thought of what she might find, she saw with relief her friend sitting up, her face bathed in sunlight, at the sound of the door, Anna turned, Belle walked toward her, on reaching the bed, she said hello Anna, then going to her friend she enveloped her in her arms, Anna's breathing sounded laboured and raw.

She could not see Belle, putting her hand up to Belle's face she stroked her face. "So Vincente couldn't be trusted." she said with a smile.

"I'm glad he can't," Belle retorted in a voice stronger than she felt, "He has given me the chance to say how much I love you."

Belle did most of the talking for the next two hours, reminiscing about their past. When Anna fell asleep, she left the room feeling exhausted. David was walking in the grounds, he found the whole place amazing, Anna had found her own utopia, leaving the house Belle caught a glimpse of David walking through the gardens, running to him she stopped just short, blurting it out, she said; Anna's blind!, she can hardly breath.

He took her hand and heading for the gate, not really knowing what he was doing; called for Vincente. Please open up he told him; we will be back in half and hour.

Although it may have been Anna's haven, David felt imprisoned. Outside the gates he spotted a bar on the far side of the square, he almost dragged Belle there; once seated he ordered two glasses of wine; he had given up smoking almost two years previously but spotting a cigarette machine, he went over and extracted a packet, the barman gave him a light.

Almost choking on the intensity, David had gone bright red and then green, Belle had imagined the last thing she would do was laugh but seeing the effect the cigarettes were having on David was hilarious, he had not realised his choice was one of the strongest on the market. As far as David was concerned if his choking gave Belle something to laugh about; he would choke some more.

They relaxed and she told him some of the history of the village, of her visits here with Anna and some devilment they got up to ten years ago when they would go to the clubs in Nerja. They had been good times, great holidays, "Halcyon days," Belle said.

When he thought she was relaxed enough David asked if it would be alright if he could visit with Anna. She felt ashamed; how she could have been so insensitive; she had not thought once of David's feelings, of course he had been Anna's friend as well; his feelings must run as deep as hers, he was glancing at her and she burst into tears again. *Shit this whole situation*; David was thinking; and he dreaded going back to the villa.

London and Maro

Enough was enough, Walters was in the foulest mood; and his sergeant couldn't get a civil word out of him. "Why didn't you tell me of this connection? Surely you could see with the phone calls and paintings something was going on?"

Sergeant Clarke looked abashed, his boss must have a good reason for being this angry; he couldn't think what, but it would eventually come to light.

Walters was angry with himself, realising as he did that the paintings on Anna's walls were, of course the same artists', he just didn't want to make the connection. *God*, he thought, *please let it be just a coincidence*, but he knew it wouldn't be. Walters went to his superior and asked if it would be possible for him to go back to Spain to follow up a connection in the Foley case; his boss knew he had just returned from holiday and thought he was pulling a fast one, no amount of explanation would get through to him, so in anger, Walters said he would go at his own expense and take extra leave if need be. His boss, intrigued, told him to calm down and start over again.

Trying to explain as patiently as though he were speaking to a child; Walters told The Chief Superintendent that the only real connection in Foley's file was the one between him buying paintings and the constant phone calls to and from the gallery. The last call he had made was to the gallery and they had discovered that the owner had left the country on the day of his murder.

Calling his wife, Walters told her to have his passport and a bag packed; he would pick them up on his way to the airport. To Walters everything was falling into place, the pity of it was, he didn't want it to.

Sergeant Clarke couldn't believe he was on a plane to Spain; his boss was sitting next to him looking out of the window and he was in the deepest depression he had ever witnessed him in. He hoped this would not go on for the whole of their stay.

The inspector left the baggage for Sergeant Clarke to pick up and made his way to the car hire desk, and by the time he had completed the paperwork the sergeant was just coming through customs. It was early evening when the two policemen booked into the Cabana Hotel on Frigata Square in Nerja.

They had a wash and change and Walters said there was a call he had to make before they would have dinner. They drove for about five minutes along the coast road out of town. Sergeant Clarke was hoping this investigation might take some time.

Inspector Walters was not looking forward to this interview if indeed he would get one. He had briefed Clarke on how ill Anna was and the fact that they may not be able to see her at all. It all seemed a bit vague and inconclusive to the sergeant until he remembered the coroners report on Foley, he had HIV; *so that was it*, the inspector thought, *this woman Anna killed Foley then ran away to Spain*, somehow it still didn't gel; in the Sergeants opinion of course.

You could have knocked Nobby Clarke down with a feather when the large black gate opened, he didn't know who was more surprised, the inspector or David Jacks. Regaining his composure the Walters stated his business and asked after Anna, and David suggested they come in.

Just as they reached the living room, Belle came in from the terrace and looked from David to the two men and back again.

David explained the inspector's visit in as few words as possible, and her temper rose to the surface, what right did they assume they had in wanting to investigate a dying woman?. There was no way she would allow Anna to be disturbed; they could get the hell out!

David had yet to be confronted by Belle's temper, and he was glad it wasn't aimed at him, but for the life of him, he couldn't understand why she was taking this attitude, but Belle's thoughts had already coincided with those of inspector Walters; Anna had left the country the day Michael Foley died she didn't want to believe it of her friend but knowing the circumstance of her impending death, and her fear at a confession on Anna's part was enough for her to try and protect Anna from herself.

Tim Walters asked Belle to please be calm and sit down. Her shoulders slumped and pursing her lips, she sat by the fireside, watching him through moisture filled eyes. Sitting opposite her, his voice softening, he explained to her how he and his wife had met Anna while they were here on holiday. She had been very kind to them both and invited them into her home, on returning to London he was surprised to find a connection between Anna and Foley and not just the telephone calls, they had discovered Foley was HIV positive, and no one outside the department knew that. Walters, knowing Anna was desperately ill, put two and two together, really all he wished to do was exclude her from his enquiry, but he needed to know if Foley had said anything to her that day on the phone that might shed some light on who he was meeting.

Belle had sat silently and listened carefully to everything he said. Closing her eyes for a few moments, she was torn between throwing them out and agreeing to them seeing Anna.

Finally she decided on the latter, perhaps because she needed to know for her own peace of mind, so rising from the chair Belle suggested the two policemen return in the morning when Anna would hopefully be a little brighter.

London

Stubbs had found the surveillance reasonably easy. His men had gained access to the houses without any problems, and the listening devices had been placed throughout the buildings, even in one man's private room at the top of his house.

This particular person loved the sound of his own voice. Around the third day of the surveillance, Stubbs was listening to the tapes from the day before, mostly this was the boring part of the job but as he listened his eyebrows drew together, and his stomach began to churn. He decided in that moment, that if Sir Geoffrey didn't go to the police with this, he would.

Stubbs decided to get in touch immediately with Tyne, instead of leaving it as he had planned, until the end of the week. Sir Geoffrey Tyne telephoned the fraud squad, he was put through to Sammy who, after listening to him for a few moments, told him they would be there as soon as possible. Sammy tried to get in touch with Walters but he was still away. Stubbs had instructions to continue with the surveillance, the man had put the rope round his own neck, now lets see how tight we can pull it.

How the hell they had missed it? Very sloppy work! Foley must have either had a brilliant mind or one of the most devious. He had lost the firm a total of £30 million, a loss they would probably never recover from.

If he had not been killed, the damage he could have inflicted on the firm would have been insurmountable. If it had not been for the astuteness of the trader who had taken over Foley's position the bonds may never have been discovered. He had managed to sell the interest payments on the lump sum of bonds but that left him with the principal portion of the same bonds. The problem was he couldn't dispose of the remainder before the interest rate went up, he had taken the risk that the market would fall before he had the chance to sell, the market collapsed and after a couple of days Foley found himself with a loss too large to admit to so he hid the bonds, probably thinking he would get rid of them at a later date.

Sammy had to find out who it was who had known about what Foley had done. On concealing the tapes to the police, Sir Geoffrey was undecided if he had done the right thing. Listening to them he had a sense of physical disgust for those who he had thought he knew; albeit, in a mainly working capacity, but he had been to this man's home, and had dinner with his wife and family.

Geoffrey Tyne was not someone who could be easily shocked but these revelations were indelible. The imagery of the words on the tapes he could not erase from his mind. Putting them into his safe, he wondered what other revelations would emerge by the time Stubbs had finished. These people needed to be stopped but Sir Geoffrey knew this was something completely out of his league.

Leaving his office he walked straight into the man whose voice he had just heard, the blood rising up to his face, he could only manage a curt nod before rushing past, he needed to get home and have a drink or be sick, or both.

Maro

Walters and Clarke had spent two days in Spain, and they were back in the office by lunchtime on the third day. In some ways the trip was one both men would rather forget.

The tableau which greeted the two policemen would be an image that would stay with them for a very long time. On entering Anna's bedroom, they both felt completely out of place, clumsy intruders unable to turn back, they stood just inside the door, with three sets of eyes boring into them, Clarke later recalled to a friend in a hushed voice how moving the scene was.

The room was bathed in bright sunlight, a nurse was sitting on the chair to the left of a large oak bed, and the doctor was standing at the end of it obscuring their view of the person lying there. Belle came toward them; she had been standing by the window. The doctor had just finished examining Anna, and Belle had seen for the first time the massive tumours covering her body, and she had to fight the bile rising into her throat.

She quickly turned to look out of the window, *God help her,* Belle was thinking. When Mia came in and announced the arrival of the policemen, Belle asked her to tell them to wait for 10 minutes.

The nurse, having prepared Anna for her visitors, resumed her position by the bed. Walking up to Walters, Belle quietly told him Anna was very weak and although she could understand what was said, she may not be able to reply to his questions. The inspector nodded his understanding.

The doctor moved over to the door, his shoulders slumping, and turning, his eyes locked with those of the inspector, their meaning transparent, it was now only a matter of hours and her pain would be over. Sergeant Clarke watched as his boss moved closer to the emaciated body lying under the stark, white sheet, he reached out and taking Anna's hand in his spoke softly to her. Asking her if she could reply to his questions with a short 'yes' or 'no', Anna replied "Yes".

Sergeant Clarke was deeply moved by his inspector's approach with the woman. When he described Anna on the drive over, he had spoken of a stunning looking woman with beautiful auburn hair, if a little on the thin side. Somehow he couldn't tally his boss's description with that of the skeletal figure lying prone on the bed.

Inspector Walters was rising from the bedside when the hand he was holding urged him back, Anna spoke a whole sentence, when she had finished her hand relaxed, the inspector leaning down kissed it. No one else in the room heard what she said and the sergeant only discovered her words when he and the inspector were on the flight home. He relayed her words to the sergeant; with an emotion he couldn't hide.

Sammy and Walters agreed to meet at the pub, its real name was the Black Swan, but to the locals it would always be the Mucky Duck, because of the amateurish painting hanging out front. This time it was Sammy's turn to wait for Tim, he was just about to go up for his second pint when he spotted him making his way through the lunchtime crowd.

He raised his hand slightly and made a drinking motion. Everything was coming together, very few stones had been left unturned by Sammy's men, and as he said to Tim Walters; there had been a peculiar incident just the day before in Tyne's office. They were discussing one name on the list when the door suddenly opened and one of the partners barged in with a face like thunder, he stopped in his tracks when he saw Sammy, and Tyne's voice was not too friendly when he asked what he wanted, but the man just blustered that he would speak to him later and stormed out.

Walters found the fact that Sammy had seen Sir Geoffrey only yesterday puzzling; he had an appointment with him at 3 o'clock, at Sir Geoffrey's own request. He wondered what Tyne wanted to say to him that could not be said to Sammy.

Sir Geoffrey Tyne's secretary showed Inspector Walters and Sergeant Clarke into his office, there was no offer of coffee this afternoon. The man himself rose from behind his desk and indicated the two chairs positioned in front of him.

When they were seated Sir Geoffrey went over to his safe, taking out the tapes, he handed them to Walters without a word. The sergeant and Walters looked at each other, reaching into his drawer Tyne produced a tape recorder and dramatically placed it in front of the two men. Taking his cue Walters slipped the tape into its position; Nobby Clarke placed his notebook on his lap and started writing.

At first it was difficult to understand, as the men were moving round the room, their voices rising and falling as they walked, there was a tinkling of glasses and then the voices became so clear they could have been in the office with them but it was the topic of their conversation which held all three of them enthralled.

They were speaking of the young boys they had enjoyed the night before and it would be a great shame if the supply were to dry up just because the supplier was no longer around. One of the men said, no one should worry about that, as he had already arranged everything, they just had to change the party venue, anyway, Foley had become troublesome, he knew far too much and was becoming a little too demanding.

The tape carried on in the same vein interspersed with bits and pieces of what could vaguely be described as family life.

Sir Geoffrey buzzed for his secretary to bring in the coffee; they all drank it wishing it were something stronger. Walters asked Sir Geoffrey where the tapes had come from, and Tyne told him all about hiring the private investigator when he realised the police could do nothing. He showed the inspector photographs of the men entering and leaving the house, unfortunately he had been unable to find out where they held the so-called parties.

Inspector Walters asked if he could keep the tapes and Sir Geoffrey was only too glad to let them go. The tapes would not be used officially but at least it gave the police a place to start, what Stubbs had done was against the strict letter of the law but Inspector Walters for one was not going to nit pick on this occasion. He had telephoned for an appointment with his chief, both he and Sergeant Clarke were loath to listen to the tapes, but knew they would be played time and time again before these men were brought to book.

The chief said he could have as many men as it would take, but they had to get this one absolutely right; once these men had been arrested there were to be no loopholes for them to slip out of. The surveillance teams were put into action; it wasn't a question of just watching the one man. They had round the clock surveillance on four men.

The team included squads from the paedophile and pornography forces, the sheer size of the operation surprised Inspector Walters. The heads of all departments were called in for consultation and it was decided the information received should be passed directly to Inspector Walters; the murder investigation was still top priority, being intermingled with a paedophile ring they hoped to kill two birds with one stone.

When Walters had arrived at Geoffrey's office, Tyne had made up his mind; Inspector Walters could have the tapes and do with them whatever he could, he, Sir Geoffrey had enough on his plate, his company, which he had helped to develop was in serious danger of going down the tubes, they were relied on for their discretion and specialist abilities when dealing with high net worth earners and he just couldn't see how the firm could ride this out; he almost wished he had never heard the dam tapes. Weller had calmed down when he saw him later that day and wanted to know what was to be done about the lost money, whose head was going to roll? His exact words were "If you're thinking that I'm going to take any of the blame for his, think again".

Sir Geoffrey just looked at him in a pitying way and dismissed him as he would have done a minion. Geoffrey Tyne had had enough, he needed to get away. The whole business had affected him badly, he had asked the police if he needed to be involved, and they had told him only if it came to court which seemed to him a long way off. At that moment he could not give a toss if the whole firm went bust, but with luck and some damage control it wouldn't. Hopefully when he returned it would all be sorted, he knew if he stayed around for much longer, he might be tempted to warn the man about the investigation.

The following day Sir Geoffrey Tyne and his wife were on a flight to America and he would not be seen back at his office for a fortnight. Sergeant Clarke, on entering the office, asked his boss if he had anything. The inspector replied the only thing he had was a bloody headache, it had been four days and nothing. All four men seemed to be acting like choirboys, not one of them had even spit on the pavement. Walters was unsure how long they could keep this up. At 9.15pm the calls started coming in, all four of them were on the move, and all heading out of town. Walters had a feeling this was it!

They headed for their cars and were directed by radio to the final destination, a large detached house in Surrey. The officer in charge of the child abuse squad told them they would have to wait at least half an hour.

"If you want evidence you need to be patient."

It was the longest half hour of Walters' life, speaking into his radio the inspector said quietly "Go! Go!" With no finesse at all 30 officers smashed their way into the front and back of the building. In the living room they found one man seated watching television and having a drink, on the screen was an image of a young boy lying naked on a bed, the man standing beside the bed was frantically trying to put his trousers back on; suddenly, his arms were pinned as the two officers burst through the bedroom door and as this was all going on, the young child lay absolutely prone.

Similar scenes were happening in four other bedrooms. When Walters and Clarke entered the house you could have heard a pin drop; the air was thick with unspoken disgust.

He walked up to one man, and speaking in a clear, resonant voice said, "Sir Brian Dunn; I am arresting you for the murder of Michael Foley. Sergeant Clarke read him his rights and get him out of my sight". The sergeant went up to Sir Brian, and pulling his arms behind his back, took great pleasure in putting the handcuffs on him, leading him past the other officers, Nobby Clarke put him in the back of a police car.

The only thing in Sir Brian Dunn's favour was that he did not plead; in fact he didn't do anything. Not one word was said by him and he kept a steely silence for the first twelve hours in custody, until, he was informed one of his compeers had decided to talk. The only thing he said was "I would like my solicitor present."

Dunn's friends were singing like canaries; they had already told Inspector Walters why Michael Foley had to die. "He was planning to expose us, and he had been demanding more money; it wasn't until after he was killed, we knew it was Brian who had murdered him!"

When Walters finally made it home late the following afternoon, he fell into bed and slept deeply for 14 hours. His wife Marie woke him and touching his face asked if it were all over, he told her of the arrests but decided to leave out the part about the children until another time.

When the police officers and social workers searched the building they found five children, all between the ages 8 and 10 years old. They looked totally bewildered; they had been taken into care and were for time being safe. Much later in the investigation the police would discover those same children were already from a care home. The man, who had been watching the television on the night of the raid, ran the home with his wife and supplied paedophiles with the young innocent children.

*

Anna's death two days after the policemen left came as a great relief to all, she had been a young woman who loved life, had given a great deal of love to those people she befriended, but by the end her friends could not bare to see her wrecked with pain. Belle had decided after the burial to stay on at the villa for a few weeks. David had phoned the gallery and asked Trish and Pat to look after things he would be back in a few weeks. The girls were in tears when he told them about Anna.

David and Belle needed those weeks; they had served as a healing process, as well as cementing their relationship. Returning to London they read in the papers about the arrest of Foley's murderer. Belle wanted to get in touch with Inspector Walters, David didn't think it was a good idea, but she said now it was all over she needed to know what Anna had said to him. Walters felt drained by everything, he should have been elated because Dunn's fellow perverts had given them all that was needed for a conviction, and Sammy had discovered Weller had been behind some very shady deals, he couldn't nail him for it but he had managed to make the man sweat a lot.

Belle rang Walters and invited him to Anna's apartment, he thought about it for a few seconds before answering 'yes'. He was still feeling very raw from the events in Spain, and still couldn't get the picture of those young children out of his mind. Perhaps talking to Belle would ease the image of Anna lying in that bed. When they were seated with a glass of red wine, Belle told him Anna had slipped into a coma the evening after he had spoken with her. Mia and Belle had sat up all the following night; she died at 4am.

"Inspector Walters", Belle said, "could you please tell me what Anna said to you? They were the last words she ever spoke".

Walters looked at her, and with an emotion he couldn't hide he said "'It's time for the artist to part with her favourite painting', and there was something else but I am afraid I didn't understand it. She said, 'The children.'"

Belle looked at him strangely, and then told him of Anna's last night at Foley's apartment. Walters said "I understand everything now".

The End